A Flower Fairy Springtime Dance

Based on the Original Flower Fairies™ Books
by Cicely Mary Barker

Frederick Warne

Deep in the garden,
a fairy is being chosen
to perform the opening
song and dance at the
Springtime Festival.

Beautiful voices and tapping
toes can be heard all around.
Eventually, it's little Narcissus
Fairy's turn.

Shy Narcissus takes her place in the clearing, as the light from a hundred stars shines down upon her.

Her twinkling toes skip delicately
across the glade. It is soon
decided that she will have the
starring role at the festival.

The fairies disappear into the dusk, leaving the Narcissus Fairy alone. "Am I really going to perform in front of all the fairies in the garden?" she asks a surprised grasshopper.

She suddenly feels frightened, so she picks up her velvety skirt and runs to the darkest part of the flowerbed.

The day of the festival dawns and the fairies are so excited.
"Where is Narcissus?" asks the Celandine Fairy. "She's the most important fairy of the day!" adds Daisy.

The Rose-Bay Willow-Herb
Fairy flys off to search for
her, but Narcissus is
nowhere to be seen.

The Crocus Fairies skip down to the pond.
"Have you seen Narcissus?" they ask a
fairy who lives nearby, but there had
been no sign of her.

At last, a passing butterfly spies Narcissus. "You must fly to the festival or you'll be late!" says the butterfly. "But I'm scared of singing and dancing on my own," whispers Narcissus.

"You'll be fine. I'll be there to watch over you," the butterfly cries. Narcissus feels much braver and soon agrees to perform.

Just as the festival begins, the smiling Narcissus Fairy confidently skips into the clearing and begins to sing and dance beautifully.

The pretty butterfly is by her side. She isn't alone after all!

At the end of the song, the fairies clap and cheer and Narcissus doesn't feel afraid anymore. She is the proudest and happiest fairy at the festival.

Her fairy friends join in the singing and dancing, and the Springtime Festival is enjoyed by all in Flower Fairyland!

FREDERICK WARNE

Published by the Penguin Group
Penguin Books Ltd, 80 Strand, London WC2R 0RL, England
New York, Australia, Canada, India, New Zealand, South Africa

This edition first published by Frederick Warne in 2006

1 3 5 7 9 10 8 6 4 2

ISBN 07232 57264

Printed in China